A DATE WITH HER DEVILS

A DATE WITH HER DEVILS

THE SEVEN SINNERS OF HELL'S KINGDOMSHORT STORY

by

GINNA MORAN

ISBN 978-1-951314-47-7 (soft cover)
ISBN 978-1-951314-48-4 (hard cover)

This is a work of fiction. All of the characters, organizations, and events portrayed in this novel are either products of the author's imagination or are used fictitiously.

Cover design by Silver Starlight Designs
Cover images copyright Depositphotos

For Inquiries Contact:
Sunny Palms Press
9663 Santa Monica Blvd Suite 1158
Beverly Hills, CA 90210, USA
www.sunnypalmspress.com
www.GinnaMoran.com

To those who love freely, endlessly, and especially with an open mind. More horns and tails for you.

Devilish Romance

RAVEN

"WHY DON'T YOU put that tail to use and hand me the lipstick." I smirk at Kase's reflection in the bathroom mirror as he stands behind me in silence.

Fire lights his eyes with his fake glare, and he tightens his arms around my waist. Watching me get ready seems to be the most fascinating thing in the world, but at least he doesn't ask to help me. He's better at smearing my makeup and would do it just to drive Dante crazy.

"I'll show you exactly how I'm going to put my tail to use if you continue to doll yourself up for those angelic bastards." He sandwiches me to the counter and uses his nose to nudge the hair from my throat. His hot lips caress my skin. "I'm starting to think you're enjoying yourself."

"I am enjoying myself," I tease, tilting my head more, showing off my throat more, silently testing to see if he'll kiss my sensitive skin again. "Now hand me the lipstick or I'll ask Dante to switch places with you."

"Fuck yeah. Move out of the way, you asshole. Raven's pouty lips are mine." Dante fills up the doorway and flexes as he clutches the frame. There isn't much room for him to barge in, but if I give him the word, he will. "You're both driving me crazy with jealousy. You know how much I desire to help her get ready."

"Because you start swearing at her brush for pulling her knotty hair," Kase quips.

"Can you blame me? That should be my job. She likes it." Dante risks Kase's wrath by stepping a foot into the tiny bathroom.

I laugh breathlessly, their banter getting to me in a good way. They love testing and teasing each other, and it helps keep things light between the three of us. And light and playful is definitely something I need. If I'm given too much silence or left to do my own thing like get ready, then my thoughts wander to all the bullshit Hell thrusts at me. Breaking angels should be fun for a Hell-bound soul, but I can't stop thinking about the absence of my first corrupted angel and how he gave up his path with the Higher Power for me.

I wish I could see him.

Then again? The last thing I want is to end up in Hell before I have a chance to fulfill my contract with Lucian. That notorious, bastard devil. I sometimes wish I could summon him and call him by his former heavenly name just to piss him off...at least from behind the protective muscular wall that Kase and Dante surround me with.

"Isn't that right, pretty-soul?" Dante asks, pulling my attention away from my deadpan expression in the mirror, staring back at me.

I shake my head with a smirk. "I get nothing out of brushing my messy hair, but if it were you pulling—"

"All right, move. You need to get dressed as well. Don't make me punish you both for causing us to be late." Striding the few feet to us, Dante towers behind Kase and wags his eyebrows.

Kase growls, revealing the blunt tips of his three horns peeking through with his half-shift into his devil form. "Don't test me, Dante, or you will be the one wearing lipstick and on your fucking knees in front of me."

Flicking out his forked tongue, Dante hisses. "What kind of threat is that? You want us to line up? Maybe I'll be on my knees for Raven instead."

My eyes widen at his remark. "Maybe you two should just go bang or something and let me finish."

The look the both of them give me sends goosebumps over my skin. I would think they had never fucked around together before.

If I hadn't had a little lesson on Blow Jobs for a Devil 101 with Dante demonstrating how Kase likes getting head, I might cringe at my joke.

"I think you've forgotten, angel-girl. You're ours. We're not going to fuck and leave you out. And now that I've fucked you how I please, Dante's ass can just wait for you to peg him. Maybe if he doesn't back the fuck off and let me watch you pucker those delectable lips of yours, I'll have you do the honors and put him in his damn place."

"Uhh, I'm okay if you do, though. So you know. Maybe." I try to remain expressionless. "Fuck, I don't know." Heat blossoms in my cheeks, and I clutch the sink. I never really thought about it until this second, and now that I can imagine it in my mind...is it weird that I don't want to be left out? Maybe I'm supposed to embody greed instead of claiming the throne of Purgatory.

"I love when she's flustered. I bet she wants to watch. Shifting behind me, Kase uses his tail and reaches for the organizer Dante put together with every damn lipstick color imaginable. He plucks a bright pink one out and dangles it in front of me. "What do you think, Dante? Bend over for a bit?"

I lick my lips and swallow, spinning around in Kase's arms. "I—"

Kissing me, Kase steals the words from my mouth and lifts me up, setting me onto the small counter. Dante towers over his shoulder, smiling with his fangs, his diamond-pupils expanding and retracting. They both know they got to me and love every second of digging under my skin.

"Relax, angel-girl. We don't have time for fucking. Dante wants to fuck you so badly that I'm not sure he could enjoy it the other way around until you let him." Kase hands Dante the slightly gaudy pink shade of lipstick without looking at him. "We'll have this conversation some other day. Right now, we have some feather-brains to check in on. Lucian's only going to give us this kind of space for so long."

"Don't listen to him. I'll devour anything you want to do with me, even a quickie. I want to know exactly what Kase gets. Especially..." His eyes flash green, his posture stiffening. "Let's just say I can't wait. You're already so good at torturing me."

He's growing jealous thinking about me and Kase together, which is one of the only reasons I haven't given in to his desperate need to get what Kase got. I'm afraid he will grow possessive, and right now, I need him to remain in control. Kase is right. I doubt Lucian will give us much time. He's probably plotting my soul's downfall because of how I bested him and managed to give myself time to force the rest of the angelic brethren to fall.

"I am getting lessons from Hell's best," I respond, snatching the lipstick from his hand. I swap it for a more neutral color and swivel on the balls of my feet, applying the best I can.

"Fuck, I want to punish you so badly," Dante mutters.

Kase swats my ass with his tail. "Later. We need you not obsessing over how sexy Raven is, especially when we need her to do her job. Knowing you, you'll chase anything with wings away."

Dante remains smiling, his demeanor still playful instead of getting angry at Kase for pointing something out. "Can you blame me?"

Kase wags his eyebrows and sneaks his hand under one of my boobs, bouncing it on his palm. "Absolutely not. I want to tear those bastards apart with my teeth."

"Give her their cocks as a gift?" Dante adds, chuckling.

"God, you guys can be psychotic. Don't you dare ever bring me a cock bouquet instead of flowers. No other body parts either. I like take-out and TV if you really want to be romantic." I squeeze past them and spin out of Kase's attempt at lassoing me with his tail. If I don't get myself together and get them to focus, we might not ever leave this apartment.

Dante rushes past me and beats us to Kase's room. Grabbing the tight, little black-sequined dress from its place on the bed, he dangles it out in front of him. "You have never truly been romanced if you haven't received something as thoughtful as a collection of cocks. Kase gave me one last century when some asshole thought he could—"

A bang on the front door of our apartment echoes through the air, cutting off what I'm sure will be some gruesome story that I'll just smile through.

Growling in unison, Kase and Dante abandon me without a word and head into the living room. I quickly slide into the extra-short dress and fix my hair, tying it up to show off the backless number with the low neckline meant to accentuate my cleavage. If Dante wasn't thoughtful enough to get me boob tape, I'd certainly end up flashing my breasts to the world at some point this evening. I already risk exposing my vagina, especially because those cute bastards whispering in the living room hide all my panties from me, saying they sent them to the cleaners.

"Are you fucking serious?" Kase's voice bellows from down the hallway. "I should end your damn contract right this second."

"Not in the living room. It took me fucking forever to clean up the blood the last time," Dante says, his comment disturbing yet completely accurate.

A guttural noise escapes from Kase. "I don't give a damn. He—"

Curling my fingers into fists, I storm toward the hallway. "Kase! Listen to Dante! I already told you I don't want to see dead guys on the floor ever again."

I reach the living room but stay just within the hallway. I don't know who exactly is with my devils, but it sounds like one of their hell-bound contracts. I know it's wrong of me, but I'd prefer to keep out of this part of their devil affairs. They've made it so easy to forget about the awful souls they have working for them and the fact that those same souls will experience eternal punishment in their levels of Hell. As long as I don't think about it, it doesn't bother me.

"Ever-ever? Because we can't promise that bullshit. What if a hoard of Hell-bound dickholes come in uninvited again and—"

"We'll take them outside to send them to Hell. Like now." Dante cuts Kase off and flashes his fangs with his smile. He whacks an unfamiliar man in the chest, knocking him onto the porch. "Pretty soul, I promise you to behave as best as I can...at least in your presence. So don't follow me. I'll be back in five."

His devilish façade breaks free, scales bursting across his skin. The man on the porch screams at a pitch only animals should be able to hear. If I didn't still have my gaze on Dante, I would have assumed he cut the man's dick off to make it the first part of a bouquet I never knew how much I didn't want until now.

"You better run, you little shit! Our fucking night is fucked up because of you," Kase snaps, shooting glowing red power out the door behind Dante.

Shit.

Sighing, I stride toward him, hoping to catch Dante. Kase blocks my way, whipping his tail around me. The world spins as he hangs me upside down by my ankles. He gives me a stern shake back and forth until my dress slides up my thighs, exposing the fact that I'm not wearing panties.

He purrs, the vibration of the feline noise buzzing across my skin. "Give me a good reason I shouldn't carry you back to Dante's room to restrain you and have my way?"

"Because that's Dante's room, and if you restrain me, it'll be for him." I squirm and tug at my dress, trying to get it back over my ass. "It sounds like we won't be going out after all, so..."

"So...you finally going to fuck the envious, desperate bastard?" Kase swings me up and catches me in his arms. "He wants you so badly, you know. I usually don't encourage being a good girl, but your kind of naughty in making him wait...thank fucking-fuck he isn't me." Chuckling, Kase adjusts me in his arms until the heat between my legs presses against his abs. He hums and lowers me even more. All it would take was a tug of his zipper, and we could fuck right here.

I clutch his face and fake-glare. "Maybe we should stop messing around until I'm ready to test Dante's envy."

Kase raises his eyebrows, his lips tilting downward as he considers my comment. "So that's it. You won't let him soak his cock in you because you're afraid his possessiveness and jealousy will get out of control."

I slowly nod, choosing not to mention that I know how much he wants to train my ass with his—I guess, our—collection of butt plugs, and I pucker thinking about anything bigger than the width of Kase's sleek tail. There is no turning back once I dive into Lubeland. That sort of intimacy isn't something I'm ready for. Dante is the master of after care and he'd...I shiver at the thought. My sweet fucking psychos. They make it hard to have a clear head.

"Partially. You know I have a job to do. One of those bastard angels is supposed to be the king of lust, so...I gotta do what I gotta do. You said it first." It should be weirder than it is, discussing how I'll continue to use my sexuality to break some righteous saviors. If my dad knew, he'd most definitely degrade me and call me something rude under his breath. But I'm not a fucking whore or slut. I'm turning into a cock collector, enjoying the fun life brings me with my devils.

Kase smirks. "As long as they earn it. And not before Dante...please."

He looks so cute and innocent with his plea that I can almost imagine him as the angel he used to be.

"I mean, it is your decision, angel-girl, but Dante is my best friend and has been through it fucking all with me. I want to experience what it's like sharing that addictive body and soul of yours with him first. It sure as shit won't be Micah's ass. The fucker still needs to be taught a damn lesson for stealing my wings." Kase's jaw twitches with his words.

I can't stop the pout puckering my lips. Not only do I wish I had more time with Micah before Lucian took him to Hell, but I also wish that Kase can eventually at least be cordial with my gluttonous devil. They will rule Hell together, and Micah got to me in a way I didn't know possible, trading his whole eternity with the Higher Power in my name because he felt his purpose changed to be me.

"By sharing, I hope you mean taking turns," I tease, forcing myself to smile. I know he totally doesn't, but I will cling onto my asshole's desire to not have the Hell fucked into it until I'm well trained and comfortable.

I shake my head, pushing the thought away. I can't believe I'm starting to accept that as part of my future, and not even as my punishment. Fuck. Me. Or should I say, double fuck me?

"Come on, angel-girl. You know the idea of our cocks boning you, slipping and sliding next to each other to possibly clap our balls together in celebration excites you. Imagine that kind of applause." He presses his lips together, trying to remain expressionless. "Hot."

I laugh in exasperation, my voice ringing through the air. "You really do want to put a hold on sex with me, don't you?"

"If it means that we get to go balls deep in a Raven sandwich, I think I can test my restraint. Shall we make a deal?" Kase sets me on my feet and rests his hands on my hips, purposefully keeping my dress hiked up. "One last bone right here and now, and then we'll wait until you're ready to fuck Dante? Unless you seduce me..."

I smack my hands into his taut chest, stopping him from assuming that my silence means I'm considering it. "You're ensuring a dry, chaste eternity, my wrathful devil. I think you've forgotten that Dante has curated an enormous toy collection just for me."

I drag my fingers down his body and glide my hands over the sharp Vs of his hips and around his waist to his lower back. His tail twitches as I lace my fingers around it, stroking my hand down the length. I pull it toward me teasing, his devilish side rubbing off on me.

"I bet he could find something to mimic your tail for me to play with," I add, biting my lip.

Kase's eyes spark with his Hell power, turning the deep, rich burgundy color red. A shadow cuts across the foyer, the silhouette of Dante's wings stretching out and then disappearing as he folds them away.

"Maybe Dante can even wear it for me. Tie me up with it." I shift on my feet and glance at the door, knowing Dante can hear. "So if you really want to make this deal…" I step back and hold out my hand. "The choice is yours."

"You naughty fucking soul. You're getting too good at making deals for my liking," Kase says.

"Sounds awesome. Take whatever the fuck deal she wants. I know exactly what I'm picking up tonight." Dante graces me with a handsome smile, his deep voice humming with playful excitement. "Might as well fill my time with something productive since our plans are fucked. I can't believe the fucking bastard insisted we split with…" He snaps his mouth shut. "This is a better backup plan than having to lure the bird brains somewhere else. Without what we need, we'll just be wasting time."

Dante purposely doesn't tell me whatever devilish business he and Kase are involved in, which means it's probably something that might make my stomach churn.

I peer at Kase and then back to Dante. I just spent the last hour or more getting ready to go out. "Uh, I bet we could think of something else. I'm dressed up and ready to go out."

Raising his eyebrow, Dante gives me a look that says he might be getting jealous of something ridiculous. "You're also dressed up and ready to stay in." He closes the space to me and cups my cheek, running his finger toward my mouth.

I whack his arm before he smears my lipstick.

Kase snuggles up behind me and teases Dante with his tail, trailing it over his scruffy chin. "I think we should take angel-girl out. Show her off. Maybe a little romancing will get her in the mood for more with you. You can impress her by showing how good you can be for her."

Dante tightens his jaw, pursing his lips. "Nobody should be graced with her beauty. The fuckers who get to see her for the first time—"

I capture his mouth with my lips, cutting off his words. He's totally putting himself in a jealous mood, his envy over thinking people seeing me for the first time is some kind of ordeal almost hysterical.

Easing away, I pucker my bottom lip. "Please, Dante. Think about how jealous every asshole who sees us together will be. They'll wish that they were me, hanging with you sexy, hot, wickedly fun devils."

Dante tips his head back and laughs, his whole face lit up by my comment. "Stop being humble. You're the most beautiful woman that has ever graced the universe. There is no possible way they'd want to be you unless it was to be able to masturbate. Because I imagine what it's like fucking yourself, and those naughty fingers of yours—fuck."

Ah, hell. "You're ridiculous," I say. "But cute and psychotically charming. Which is why I'll make you a deal."

"If we take you out on a date, we'll end the night getting to fuck you together," Kase says, pushing his hard-on to my ass.

I shake my head.

"Her ass isn't ready yet," Dante says before I can respond.

I squeeze my eyes shut, heat blooming across my cheeks.

"A date night, some ass play to get you nice and ready, and then double dicks?" Kase twines his tail around my leg, working his way up to my thigh.

I lock him out by crossing my legs. "Take me out, and I'll let Dante smear my lipstick how he wants before taking a bubble bath with him."

"Add in wash your hair, and it's a deal." Dante grins and holds up his hands.

Kase growls. "Hey, that's not—"

I slide my fingers through Dante's fingers. "Deal."

"Fuck yeah." Dante engulfs me in a hug, lifting me off my feet. He snatches Kase by the shoulder and pulls him closer. "Hurry the hell up and finish getting ready. I can't wait."

Quirking his lips, Kase offers me a smile and smacks my ass in Dante's arms. "You're lucky I'll have a day with you tomorrow, angel-girl. You're going to need hot tea for your throat and some ice for your knees."

"It'll be worth it," Dante says, kissing my neck. "No other date with a mortal asshole will compare. Your standards are going to be set at heights even angels can't reach."

Who knew how much I'd want a date with my devils?

I smile. "I can't wait."

Chapter 2

Divine Interference

Kase

"A LIMO? SERIOUSLY?" Raven clutches both mine and Dante's hands, staring at the driver rushing around the trunk to open the back door. "I thought you guys preferred to drive."

I guide her forward, motioning to Dante to enter first to help her inside the sleek, black vehicle. "Only I like to drive, and I can't do what I want if I have to focus. Dante shouldn't be the only one who gets to eat." I flick my tongue at her, loving how blush warms her cheeks at my insinuation. We both know I don't eat human food.

"Yeah, pretty soul. Every date should start off with a delectable dinner, and you're the only thing we crave." Dante pulls Raven onto his lap and kisses her bare neck. His fangs graze over her skin, and she shivers.

The driver shuts the door in silence and heads toward the front. I adjust the curtain over the partition, blocking his view, though he knows well enough not to try to peek or listen in for that matter.

I slide into the seat across from Dante and Raven, wanting to stare at them straight on."

"Are you trying to ensure we never leave the limo?" Her words come out breathlessly.

A wicked grin crosses my face. "Perhaps. It'll determine if our destination is good enough if you choose it."

"Unless she just wants to let me eat her for dessert there." Dante shifts his hands to massage his fingers into her smooth, bitable thighs. "I can already taste you, pretty soul."

Raven gasps at his touch, squirming in an attempt to resist how he spreads her legs, giving me the best view of her naked body. He's right about tasting her. My mouth waters at just the thought of gliding my tongue over her smooth lips to enjoy her sweet pussy. The devil inside me purrs, and I unwind my tail from my back and lace it around her wrists, keeping her from trying to touch herself in anticipation.

"Kase," Raven murmurs, a soft groan of a whimper escaping her pouty mouth.

"You want me now, don't you?" I grin as I move forward, getting on my knees between the seats. "Tell me, Raven. I want to know that this is how you'd love to start off our date."

She hums and bites her lip, rolling her hips against Dante's lap. Her desperation for pleasure tightens my nuts, my cock throbbing for the chance to sink inside her. Dante continues to kiss her throat while gliding one of his hands from her thigh and between her legs.

He taps two of his fingers to her clit, making her gasp and arch her back. "Tell him."

"I want you, Kase," she says, moaning. "Waiting is torture."

"Let me see if you're telling the truth." I rest my warm hands on her knees, slowly running them along her legs upward to her thighs.

Holding Raven's heavy-lidded gaze, I watch her expression as I dip my finger between her legs, feeling her slick excitement, her body craving me as much as her mind and soul. I bring my finger to my lips and suck it into my mouth, humming at her sweetness. Dante's eyes flicker green, his envy flaring.

"Do you want a little taste of our woman, Dante?" I ask him. I love testing his resolve, getting him to keep his jealousy and possessiveness in check, but I also know how addicted he is to her, and I don't mind giving him a fix to hold him over until he gets his turn.

Raven moans again, tipping her face toward the tinted sunroof. Taking my time, I finger her over and over until Dante looks ready to snatch my hand. Raven pants and watches as Dante sucks my finger into his mouth. She loves seeing us together. Loves being with us.

"Our perfect, beautiful soul, right Dante?" I ask him, stretching up to kiss Raven. "Tell her how she tastes."

A bright flash of heavenly light sets the cabin aglow as a fucking angel flies overhead. The bastard thinks he's damn sneaky, but with Raven's soul in our hands, we can see him when he chooses to reveal his presence to her. And why now?

"Fuck," Raven says, twisting free from my tail and managing to stretch her legs to close them, not letting Dante keep her in place.

I growl, her reaction the exact reason the bastard angel decided to make himself known. He's probably been following us since we left the apartment.

"Do you think he's going to attack us?" Raven scoots off of Dante's lap and away from the sunroof, her face blazing red from her wild emotions.

"Attack, no. Try to cock-block, yes." A growl escapes my lips as I narrow my gaze on the stingingly bright light of angel wings. I can't tell who the hell it is, but it doesn't matter. I'll fuck him up for ruining our attempt to romance Raven. "I'm going to tear his damn wings off."

Raven puffs out a breath and crosses between seats to get by my side. Hugging her arms over my shoulders, she hugs me and grazes her lips to my ear. "Why don't we just use this to our advantage? Show him what he's missing."

Dante groans. "You're going to fuck Kase in front of the angel? Damn, pretty soul. What do I have to do to be the lead in that fucking show?"

Raven shakes her head, whipping her black hair around with her high ponytail. "I'm not having sex with anyone in front of Andre."

Of-fucking-course it's Andre. Raven told us that she suspected that he could be the one to fall by lust with how easy it was for her to get him to drop his pants and nearly stick his dick in her mouth all because she said that's how he could make her feel better. I know the righteous asshole isn't that naïve. He was happy to play along with her. The fucker.

Stretching her hand to Dante, she wiggles her fingers and gets him to take it. "And that's not how I want to do it with you. Not with an audience."

A soft smile tilts up the corners of Dante's lips. Raven's got a tight grip on his nuts and he doesn't even know it. At least he'll get an amazing fucking blowjob come the end of the night. That sexy, pouty mouth of hers can take more than I ever expected. She's the queen of fucking deep-throating, if there was such a thing, like she was made for us.

Dante caresses his finger along her lip line. "You're right. I don't want that either. I need to have you all to myself when you're ready. I'll give you everything you want from start to finish."

He sounds romantic, but I know him like we share a damn brain, and I bet he's fantasizing about tangling his fingers in her hair while fucking her face. Maybe even blow his load on her tits, because he knows better than to cum in her mouth before my time. She'd be too high to do anything because his cum shares whatever the fuck chemicals that his venom does.

"The wait will be fucking worth it," he adds, making Raven smile.

It takes everything in me not to comment. Patience isn't my strong suit, so I don't get his reasoning. I mean, waiting to screw when we could fuck all-day, every-fucking-day? Now that's worth not waiting. But whatever makes him feel better. Now that I know for certain Raven is just nervous and not changing her mind about wanting to be with both of us, I'm here for whatever she wants. She's our soul forever.

Raven leans over and kisses Dante, letting him get carried away by slipping his tongue in her mouth. I could let him have his moment, but fuck it. I want in on the action, since the bastard feather-head ruined my chance to make her squirt all over my damn face. It would've been fucking awesome. Hot. Son-of-a-bastard. I want her.

Locking my fingers into Dante's hair, I shift his face to make room for me. Raven is caught off guard that I don't bother stealing her and instead slip my tongue along both of theirs that she intakes a breath, allowing us both to taste her. She loves it. Fuck, Dante loves it. The talented bastard splits his tongue and gives me part of his attention.

Easing away from us, Raven grins, her eyes crinkling in the corners. I try to kiss her again, but she grabs my tail and makes me jump. The naughty soul. She knows exactly how to wrap me around her with just the squeeze of her hand.

"That was...fucking fun," she says. Laughter bubbles from her mouth, and she fans her face, hot with her desire.

"So why stop, angel-girl?" I say, winding my tail around her wrist. I tug her closer and slide my fingers into her hair.

She turns her head like the tease she loves to be, avoiding getting distracted by what my mouth does to her. "I think we're here—wherever that is. The driver just parked."

"We're in no hurry," Dante says, caught up with his own lust and need.

"What if Andre leaves?" Raven presses her lips together, trying and failing to remain expressionless. She knows that bastard is going to be a fun bitch to break, but damn it. This is our date night.

I swallow my own jealousy and anger over Andre's surprise arrival. He's not a damn threat to us, and Raven isn't interested for the sake of just being able to say she broke a bunch of angels. She's in this because her soul and eternity are at risk to be enslaved by Lucian. Our future in changing Hell lies with her doing whatever it takes. We've all agreed that this job could mean Raven falling for others. I know how much she likes Micah and is eager for Lucian to finally release him.

"Raven's right, Kase. We have to keep things interesting." Dante wags his eyebrows.

"Fucking fine." I was already going to agree, but if Dante can be the good big devil for Raven, then I can play my part as the stubborn ass who can be worn down.

Pulling my tail from Raven's hand, I knock on the partition, getting the driver's attention. He hustles to get the door for us and looks relieved we're leaving. I should be offended, but I do own the guy's soul. I rather enjoy seeing him on edge.

I peer around, spotting Andre soaring above. His annoying bright wings ruin the view of the cityscape for Raven. She can't take her eyes off him, tilting her head toward the sky. At least he doesn't have telepathic powers. Drives me crazy that she has that sort of connection with Micah. I wish I could hear her thoughts. Fuck, I'm sounding like Dante.

Grabbing her face between my palms, I ease her focus back to me. "Lesson number one for the night: stop giving him your attention. We want him to feel like a mere mortal in your presence."

"Yeah, we know he's hot, and you obviously enjoyed seeing his cock with how you described it when I asked, but he needs to feel like nothing tonight. Make him want to be one of us." Dante laces his fingers through Raven's and tugs her away from me and beside him.

"Also, shake that damn bubble butt of yours. Bend over and give him a tiny peek." I smack her ass before falling into step beside her, draping my arm over her shoulders protectively.

"Most importantly, let us show you a good time. Fuck everything else going on. I've arranged the best of the best tonight." At least it better fucking be. One of my contract's asses is on the line otherwise. Raven doesn't have to know that though.

"You know I'm happy with whatever. I just love going out with you two. It's been so long since I've had a date," Raven says, slipping her hand under my jacket and across my lower back. The tease.

I grin, watching Raven's eyes light up as we enter the lobby of one of Angel Canyon's most luxurious hotels with an exclusive rooftop club. Music, dancing, and bottle service should get Raven's blood pumping, but not only that, I had a bottom feeder bastard call upon one of his contracted souls to guarantee an extra surprise for the night.

"Misters SaTan, Ms. Rose. Welcome to Night Tower Plaza." The concierge greets us with a smile, his eyes devouring Raven as she stands tucked between us.

Dante tightens his jaw and glances at me. "Why don't you take our girl up? I'll get everything settled."

I nod and don't waste another minute. I have a feeling that Dante's pissed at the concierge for even looking at Raven and wants me to get her away. He probably also plans to see what he can get out of the soul, obviously into something dark enough to streak the fucker's soul in shadows.

Raven remains quiet until we reach the gleaming golden door of the elevator. "SaTan? You use fucking Satan as your last names?" Her shoulders shake with her laughter.

"You love it, don't you? You can't do anything these days without one. It has always been a bit of a joke. Why does Lucian get to always be the fucking notorious Satan? So can we." I wait for the elevator doors to close and spin her around, propping her up against the wall. I kiss her softly, keeping myself in check.

She pats my shoulders. "So, Mr. SaTan." She smirks, emphasizing the T like the concierge had done. "What kind of date do you have planned? A romantic night in with room service? Because I'm not so sure that's going to tempt Andre to the devilish side."

I suck her bottom lip between my teeth, not answering her right away. "The suite is for later." The elevator jolts to a stop and the door slides open, giving us a view of a swanky check-in counter with a woman in all black with gaudy jewelry standing behind it. "Right now, we're going to Pleasure."

"Pleasure?" Raven lifts an eyebrow.

I wink at her and greet the hostess with only my name for our reservation. "You'll see."

Music pulsates through the air, humming through the glass door leading to the club with a rooftop view of the city. Red lights glow in long strands overhead, giving the place the seductive vibe of its namesake. People pack onto the dancefloor in the middle of VIP booths. A bar with shelves of liquor lit in dim lighting takes up the side with the door to the elevator, and on the other, a glass-floored viewing deck behind a chain holds a few tall tables with stools.

"This is incredible!" Raven shouts, raising her voice over the music.

I take her hand and spin her around, guiding her to the dance-floor. As much as I don't want these disgusting, sweaty mortals within an arm's reach of Raven, I can tell how excited she is by the thought of dancing. I won't deny her what she desires, not for my own selfish reasons. Turning her back to me, she drops low and pops her sexy ass back up, grinding her spankable bubble butt against my cock. And for fuck's sake. I should be used to my eternal boner for her. I just got my dick to chill out and stop threatening the strength of my pants, and Raven had to go and rub the beast awake.

It's going to be a long night if she doesn't let me fuck her in one of the shadows.

"Fucking hell. How are you managing not to tear that bastard—" Dante presses his chest to my back. "And that dickhole. The bitch-boy, and that mother fucker to pieces? His elbow grazed hers."

Hooking my arms around Raven, I lift her and swivel, setting her between me and Dante. I don't have a chance to respond to him because Raven jumps and flings her arms around his neck, getting him to pick her up for a kiss.

"This is the best. Seriously. You have no idea how much I love dancing. Joel hated it." Raven wiggles until Dante relents and lowers her to the floor.

Just the mention of Raven's bastard ex sends heat boiling through me.

"Add that to his eternal punishment," Dante says, staring at me over Raven's head.

She laughs, not even fazed—or maybe she doesn't realize it—by how serious Dante is. "I'm sorry. I didn't mean to bring him up. I'm just—you two are the best. I love it."

"Enough to let me fuck you over there?" I hum and motion toward the side of the bar at an empty pathway that wraps around the rooftop. "Dante will ensure no one bothers us."

Crinkling her nose, she shakes her head, whipping her ponytail. "Not quite. I don't want to leave him out either. It's our date."

Dante scoops Raven up, grinning like a cocky fucking bastard. "This is why I'm so obsessed with you, pretty soul. You know exactly how to make a devil feel wanted."

"You are wanted," she says. "Both of you. Forever."

"I think that might deserve a toast. Come on. These lowly mortals have had enough of your irresistible presence." I nudge Dante with my fist, getting him to carry our soul from the dance floor. "It's time for some bottle service and a little surprise for you."

"A surprise?" Raven asks, stretching her neck to look at me.

I caress her cheek with my fingers. "You'll see."

Chapter 3

Her Soul to Keep

DANTE

M Y FUCKING BALLS ache.

When we decided to take Raven out on a date, I hadn't thought about the impact it would have on my cock. The fucking thing throbs with desire, wanting to bust out of my pants. If my belt didn't restrain it in this uncomfortable position with my damn tip threatening to poke out from my pants, it'd be the ultimate weapon. I could bat all the sweaty, entitled souls thinking that they're worthy to be within a foot of Raven away with a swing of my hips.

I consider it as we walk toward the secluded sky deck meant for the elite. I could summon as much wrath as Kase in Raven's honor and bring punishment to those in our vicinity. This is why I prefer to go to places we own and have our legions run. The patrons know the rules. No looking. No touching. If they break a rule, I can take their heads.

But this is an ordinary mortal club and I have to suck up my desire to inflict punishment. For Raven's sake. I know she's iffy on that shit, and I don't want to turn her off me. I haven't had the chance to get her addicted to my devilish cock to where she doesn't care that I do what is necessary in regards to the damned. It's not like they don't deserve it.

"This is insane." Raven wiggles and squirms in my arms, rubbing her body along the length of my shaft.

I groan and set her down, the sensation of her grinding testing my resolve. I want to bend her over and fuck her so badly that I have to step back and press my palm to my boner to control myself.

She grabs my arm, reconsidering standing on the glass floor. "And a bit scary. You both better keep your devils in check. If this glass shatters under your power—"

"I'll catch you," I say, interrupting her. Flashing my wings for a split second, I remind her how safe she truly is.

"What about the others?" Raven gives me a pointed look, her lips twisted as she waits for my reply. She expects me to say screw the others, but I plan to surprise her.

"I'd save them all. We can't have one of the stars of your favorite show's splatter on the street below, now can we?" I grin, showing off my fangs. Flicking out my tongue, I hiss lowly in anticipation to her reaction. I had to rewrite a contract to make this happen, and the showrunner is one lucky bastard. I've freed his soul upon his death to go wherever the hell it goes. It's highly doubtful he could recover even an ounce of good standing with the Higher Power with his record, but he won't get punished in my level. What the fuck ever. It's worth it seeing the recognition soften Raven's features as her pouty mouth drops open.

"Oh, my God," she says, staring at some mortal who goes by Tanya Heartbreaker instead of Carin Smith, the name that'll surely end up on some demonic contract within the year. "Is that...? Oh, fuck. It is. And she's with—shit. Damn. I can't believe—"

"Take a breath, angel-girl," Kase says, grabbing her face, getting her to turn away from the reality star and back to him. "I'm starting to regret our surprise, especially with you dropping blessed words to burn my ears."

Her eyes dart away from his, though she doesn't turn her head. "Fuck, I'm just—I've never seen anyone famous before."

Play-growling, he waves his hand up and down himself. "Hel-lo?"

Raven tips her head back with a melodious laugh, her voice ringing over the thudding music. I can't help getting caught in her wild emotions and chuckle.

Grabbing Kase's shoulder, I give him a shake. "She said famous, not infamous."

"Yeah, Kase. You know I—" Raven snaps her mouth shut, dipping her chin to stare at the glass floor beneath us.

Soft light illuminates below, and I catch sight of Andre standing on the ledge of a window, peering up.

"What the fuck?" Raven says, shifting on her feet.

Kase bellows a laugh and spanks Raven's ass. "The bastard. Of course he chose to watch us from below. He's enjoying the show." Sneaking his tail out from beneath his jacket, Kase slides it under the hem of Raven's dress, reminder her that she's panty-less and giving the lusty dickhole one helluva show.

My cock pulses at the thought.

Fucking glass.

I'm now jealous of not only Andre, but the floor.

"Come on, angel-girl. Show him what he craves. He showed you his cock," Kase adds, kissing her bare throat. "He could choose to jump from grace this instant if you do."

Raven sucks in her bottom lip, considering his words instead of brushing him off. Tingles course over my skin, my muscles rippling and flexing. Damn it, what I wouldn't give to join the bastard below just for a small show of Raven's smooth, wet, fucking delicious pussy I want to bury my face in all day.

"Tanya! Tanya, you fucking bitch! I knew it!" A masculine voice bellows through the night, whipping my attention from the dancing lights on the glass, finally landing on the right spot to create a reflection where I can see exactly what I want.

"Sir, step back." A bouncer straightens his back, blocking the man from entering the sky deck.

"I'm not fucking stepping back. Do you know who I am? That's my wife!" the man shouts.

"Fuck," Raven whispers under her breath, devouring the shit unfolding before us.

I smile and squeeze her hand, watching the lights dance across the beautiful blue-green depths of her eyes. I couldn't have asked for a more perfect coincidence, like the stars align to give Raven exactly what she needs, seeing the drama she enjoys watching on TV in gluttonous amounts set the club abuzz.

"Let's grab a seat and some drinks," Kase says, chuckling as the bouncer shoves the man back. "I'll have a shot just for you."

Neither of us eats or drinks but it's not because we can't. We just don't need to.

"I can't believe Kenneth's here. There are not even cameras around. This has to be real, right? You guys didn't hire them?" Raven blindly follows Kase as he tugs her to a high table and pulls out a barstool for her.

"Nah, pretty soul. We couldn't make this shit up. Mortals like them are natural disasters," I say, sliding up behind her stool to rest my arms over her shoulders.

"Tanya!" the man shouts again. "Face me!"

Kase releases a guttural growl, spotting the man reach inside his jacket. Unfurling my wings, I wrap them around Raven and shield her protectively. The naughty soul has the nerve to grab the top of my wing and push it down, taking a peek.

"Shit. Someone do something," Raven says, realizing the man pulls out a gun.

"Miracles aren't our forte, angel-girl." Kase's devil form ripples beneath his skin, threatening to break free. As much as we want to play the heroic part for our soul, we can't. The asshole doesn't have a demonic contract. He isn't even hell-bound. If one of us chooses to intervene and stop him when Raven isn't the one being threatened, it could fuck things up.

"If we stop him, he won't get marked for Hell. He might even use the damn moment to reflect on his decisions and change his fate," I say, tightening my wings around Raven.

"What?" Raven asks. "He's not Hell-bound?"

I puff a breath against the back of her ear. "Nope. If Andre wants to intervene and change his destiny—"

Sliding off the barstool, Raven drops out of the protection of my wings and kneels on the floor. She peers down and knocks her fists on the glass, showing Andre that she knows he's standing there like an angelic creep.

"Andre! Andre, help! You can help!" Raven yells, though her words get lost in the screams and panic breaking out in the club.

Spreading his wings, Andre launches from the ledge and takes flight. He soars upward toward us, his hands sparkling with golden light.

I don't believe it.

The fucker might actually help.

A scream rings through the air, and I drag Raven from the floor and into my arms. Heavenly light bursts in the sky above as more saviors come into view. But this isn't divine intervention. This is the fuckers trying to take advantage of the chaos. I knew they wouldn't give up on trying to get Raven, but her soul is ours to keep.

A gunshot pops, blasting through the night. I cringe and spin with Raven, preparing to launch into the sky.

"Fuck it. If those bastards want to fucking do something, I'll give them something to do. Get ready to take our girl inside, Dante. I'm not letting them ruin our date." Kase roars, unleashing his devil form, turning into the powerful sexy beast he is.

I adjust Raven in my arms and stride toward the end of the sky deck and away from the chaos that comes to a halt as Kase lands next to the man and bouncer, fighting over the gun. Losing one soul to the saviors will be worth it now that they'll have to clean up the damn mess. They prefer to remain elusive and hidden within their light, but they will take the damn credit to ensure the mortals don't start thinking we're the good guys.

What the fuck ever. I don't give a shit. All I want is to get Raven out of here and enjoy the rest of our night together.

"I think I'm done here. I prefer our alone time," Raven says, nervous laughter turning her voice breathless.

"Sorry if the night was ruined, but I'd love to make up for it," I murmur, hugging her tightly. I launch from the sky deck and into the air, only flying a few feet to land near the door to the elevator down.

Silence fills the air as the angels slow the world, getting the chaos in control. I don't wait to see if they pick a fight with Kase and carry my beautiful woman inside, refusing to let her go until I kick open the door to our penthouse suite with the same amazing view as Pleasure. But here, we're going to truly fall to our deepest, darkest desires.

Raven wiggles and shifts, trying to peer around the penthouse as I stride across the living room and to the master suite. An arched doorway shows off the pleasantly gigantic bathroom with a Jacuzzi tub on a textured stone platform. The walk-in, dual headed shower glistens with mirrored fixtures and opaque glass walls, inviting me toward it. As much as I want to sink into the tub with Raven, I know Kase should arrive any minute, and it's better not having to fight him over who holds our soul.

"Dante, you're not going to let me look around?" she exclaims, her voice light and airy, filled with excitement.

"After I wash your hair. I want nothing more than to bathe every inch of you and rinse away the remnants left behind of the mortals from the club." I set her ass on the edge of the tub and flick on the hot water. "I can't stand that they got to share your breathing space."

She giggles and slides off the counter, bunching my dress shirt in her hands. "You're too much sometimes. I don't know what I'm going to do with you."

I chuckle. "I can think of a few things, pretty soul."

She surprises me by using her devilish strength to rip my shirt open, sending my buttons flying every which way. Her sudden control over me prods at my deep-seated nature to dominate her as my soul, but I want to see what she has in store for me even more.

Dropping to her knees, she unfastens my belt, grinning up at me from her place on the tiles. My cock throbs, pulsing in anticipation as my pants loosen, and she flicks open the button and nearly gets whacked by my boner because I'm going commando like she is. She gasps and laughs in surprise, clutching my hip as she readies herself, unfazed by the surprise release of my dick.

"You're so fucking hard, Dante." Tugging my pants to my ankles, Raven cups my balls, rubbing her thumb over my smooth skin.

"What are you going to do about it, Raven?" I cover her hand with mine, getting her to glide her slender fingers over the length of my shaft.

She glides her pink tongue over her lips, turning her gaze from mine to my cock, watching the pre-cum glisten from my tip. Leaning forward, she parts her mouth and flicks her tongue over my head, tasting me in response to my question.

"Mmm," she hums. "My tongue tingles."

I twist her ponytail in my hand, guiding her to suck me deeper into her mouth. "You like the taste?"

"So good." Her eyes hold mine, and she watches me watch her.

She is so fucking sexy on her knees, stretching her mouth and deep-throating me. It's like her body was made to be ravished by a devil when others would gag.

"Don't you fucking cum in her mouth, Dante. I can't fuck her how I like if she's high on your darkness," Kase's gruff voice snaps from behind me. "You hear that, angel-girl? No swallowing."

I clutch Raven's hair, keeping her from pulling away to respond to Kase, and she hums her response instead, bobbing her head faster and faster, the wet slickness of her spit, the sensation of her tongue, and how she fucking knows exactly how to play with my balls ignites indescribable pleasure through me.

My body hums as my cock prepares to explode. And damn. I nearly get her to slow down but I'm dying for some relief from the torture she puts me through by just standing next to me all day without bending over to let me fuck her.

Scales blossom on my arms, my true body breaking free from my human façade. "Pretty soul, I'm going to cum," I warn her, flashing my fangs. Releasing her hair, I reach down and tear the front of her dress right down the middle, sending it pooling at her hips.

Raven's eyes widen for a split second, but not in fear. Easing away, she continues to work me over with her hand, using her spit to rub and tug me until I grunt, my muscles tightening, and I cum all over the cleavage of her big tits threatening to burst through the flimsy fabric of her bra.

I can't stand not seeing her naked, so I tear off her bra too, leaving her panting and grinning at me from her place on the floor. "Are you ready for me to take care of you now, Raven?" I ask her, tugging her hair from her ponytail, letting it spill over her shoulders.

She licks her lips and glances from me to Kase. "What about you?"

Kase's eyes light with his devil power as he strips down, piling his clothes on the floor. Stroking his cock, he whips his tail around her, pulling her to her feet. "First, I'm carrying you into that hot shower and you're going to sit on my lap how I want." He smirks at me and winds his tail around my waist, yanking me closer at the same time he slips the tip of his tail along my ass crack. "And then you're just going to have to wait and see. One thing is for certain, though. You're not the only one going to have bruised knees."

Raven gasps with a laugh, startling under the strength of his palm as he spanks her ass, getting her to move toward the shower. My cock already hardens again, anticipation coursing through me. Steam fills the air, glistening over my skin. Kase does exactly what he says, grabbing Raven by the hips and dragging her to his lap.

"Make sure she's nice and ready, Dante," he commands, taking charge like he enjoys. I relent, unfazed by his demands.

"Only if she makes sure you're nice and slick for me," I tease, grinning at the two people I want and desire most in the world. Raven is our girl to enjoy and share, to take care of and protect, and give her the eternity as our queen as she deserves. In this moment, I don't fucking care about anything else.

"Spit, angel-girl. Dante wants to be fucked too." Kase brings his tail to her pouty mouth.

I stare at her, watching her reaction, remaining expressionless. For the first time, I worry that she might get jealous that Kase might give me a piece of his demonic glory too.

Her eyes flick to mine as she processes his comment. "Yeah? You'd like that?"

"If you're willing to share," I say.

Grabbing Kase's tail, she glides her tongue over it and wets it with her saliva. Kase moans under the sensation of her mouth, and I get down and kneel between their legs. Lifting Raven up, Kase tests her body with his tip, giving me the hottest view of his cock teasing our girl. I moan and bow forward, flicking my tongue over her clit, ensuring she gets exactly what she wants as she creams for the both of us.

"How does she taste?" Kase asks, sliding deeper into her as I lick her sweet pussy, rubbing her clit between the fork of my tongue.

"Like pure ecstasy," I murmur.

Raven moans and clutches my head, combing her fingers into

my hair. "Feels like it too."

"Ready for me too, Dante?" Kase asks, his voice deep and breathless as his tail grazes my thigh, gliding toward my ass. "Because I'm ready for you."

My nuts tighten and I moan at the sensation of Kase's tail getting me in the spot that makes me feel like I'm going to cum all over again. The three of us fall silent, though our moans and pleasure fill the air with our passion. Raven watches me on my knees, her mouth pouty, her nipples hard as pebbles despite the heat of the shower and our bodies.

Raven's body tenses and she screams with her orgasm, and I savor the rush of her squirting on me just how I crave. She grabs my shoulder, begging for me to come closer, and she strokes her fingers over my boner, jerking me off again while I transform just enough to change the texture of my hand to rub over her clit with my scales.

"I'm going to fucking explode. Brace yourself, angel-girl," Kase mutters, moaning and scrunching his face.

I extend my fangs in anticipation, yearning to see Raven's bliss as he fucks the Hell into her. Raven screams in pleasure again, leaning forward and sinking her teeth into my shoulder at his powerful orgasm. The burst of good pain shocks through me, and I shudder and fucking cum again.

Sinking against Raven, I sandwich her to Kase, imagining how damn amazing it's going to be when I can finally fuck her too. But right now? I'm good. I'm incredible. This date with our pretty soul was exactly what I needed to help clear my mind and give me the strength I need to do anything and everything it takes to ensure Raven's soul is ours forever. Not a damn angel, not Lucian, no one, will mess things up for us. I'll burn the world down if they even try.

Kase and I give Raven all the affection she craves through the rest of our shower, and I carry her in my arms to the bed we'll share for the rest of the night.

"I'm sorry things didn't go exactly as we planned, pretty soul," I murmur, settling beside her on the king-sized bed.

"It was still the best date I've ever had." She snuggles close. "It makes me want to fight even harder. Break every damn angel, no matter what it means. I don't need my soul free from Hell, but just from Lucian. My soul belongs to you."

"And we belong to you too." I lean in and kiss her softly.

Kase pops the cork on a bottle of champagne, offering it to Raven as he lies on her other side. "We'll bend things to our will in no time. I mean, look. That bastard still can't keep away."

I peer out the window at Andre soaring through the sky nearby. Two other forms light up the night above him. "None of them will be able to resist."

Raven nods her head and leans back on the pillows. "I can't wait for those bastards to take their damn thrones."

I smile at her and Kase. "Hell will be ours. And soon."

Other RH Books

OMEGAVERSE SERIES

Saint Vista Pack Regimes

Bonds of Steele Omegaverse

PARANORMAL

The Seven Sinners of Hell's Kingdon

The Pack Mates of Lunar Crest

The Wolfpacks of Shadow Moon Island

The Fated Mate of the Dragon Clans

The Divine Vampire Heirs

The Royale Vampire Heirs

The Academy of Vampire Heirs

La Vega Vampire Showstoppers

Rise from the Flames

About Ginna Moran

GINNA MORAN IS the *USA Today* Bestselling author of over seventy novels including the popular Knotty Lessons and The Seven Sinners of Hell's Kingdom novels.

She always carried a fascination for all things paranormal and wrote her first unpublished manuscript at age eighteen. Her love of the supernatural grew stronger through her adult life, and she now spends her days with different creatures of the night. Whether it's vampires, werewolves, dragons, fae, angels, demons, or mermaids, Ginna loves creating and living in worlds from her dreams.

Aside from Ginna's professional life, she enjoys binge-watching TV, crafting and design, playing with her daughter, and cuddling with her dog. Some of her favorite things include chocolate, mermaids, anything that glitters, learning new things, cheesy jokes, and organizing her bookshelf.

www.ingramcontent.com/pod-product-compliance
Lightning Source LLC
Chambersburg PA
CBHW061501210726
48287CB00007B/2611